Be brave

要勇敢

Tiger! Tiger! Tail on Fire!

Written by Lin Fong-O'Neill

Illustrated by Ray Yuen

Written by Lin Fong-O'Neill
Illustrated by Ray Yuen

ISBN: 0-9786441-1-5

Library of Congress Control Number: 2007902300

Published by Ben-Lin Associates Ltd.
P.O. Box 53, Colts Neck, New Jersey 07722   USA

Cover, Illustrations and Book design by Ray Yuen
Edited by Alexandra Leroy, Hope and Troy O'Reilly

Printed in China by Everbest Printing Co.
through Four Colour Imports, Louisville, Kentucky   USA

For my nieces, Betty, Elizabeth,
and Jennifer Fong - Lin

To all my friends spread far afield,
"Wish you were here." - Ray

Once upon a time in a far away place, there lived a small family.

Mommy, Betty and Penny made a happy home.
But Betty, being very tiny for her age, sometimes felt insignificant.

One afternoon Mommy left for the market with Penny. She reminded Betty not to open the door to strangers.

On their way Mommy and Penny met a tiger.
He was celebrating his birthday by himself.

Tiger asked where they were going.

"To get apples to make Betty's favorite pie," said Mommy, trembling.

"Who's Betty?" asked Tiger.

"My daughter."

Tiger squinted his eyes. "Yummm... a delicious family to eat on my birthday! Let me go get Betty."
Mommy let out a cry and Penny barked nervously.

Tiger tied up Mommy and Penny after he pulled off Mommy's jacket.
"Betty may be little," said Mommy, trying to remain calm, "but she's
not afraid of you."
Penny agreed with a "Woof! Woof!"

Tiger swiped at the air with his big paws and roared, "What?
Not afraid of me, the most powerful creature in the universe?"
Angrily, he set off to find Betty.

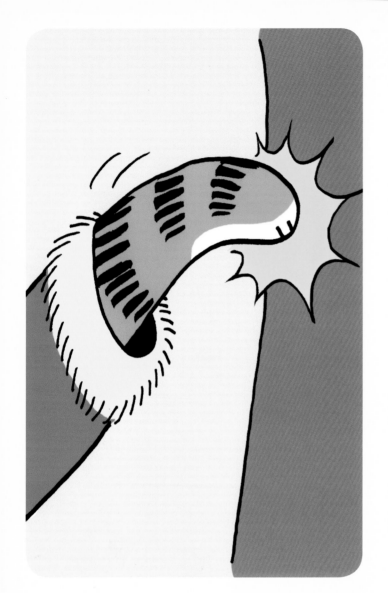 

At the door, Tiger called out in a woman's voice, "Open up!
Mommy's home!"
Betty peeped through a crack in the door and saw only Tiger's waist.
"My mom doesn't have such a big stomach," she said.
"Betty, it's Mommy!" growled Tiger. "I ate a few donuts at the market.
That's all."

Unconvinced, Betty climbed on a chair to look through the peephole.

She saw a little bit of Tiger's face.

"My mom doesn't have such a big nose," she said.

"I got stung by bees!" Tiger hollered. "It hurts. Now let me in!"

"Oh, poor Mommy..." Betty opened the door.

Tiger entered and revealed himself, roaring.
"Please!" Betty cried. "Don't hurt me!"
She was very frightened indeed, especially when she saw Tiger
wearing Mommy's jacket.

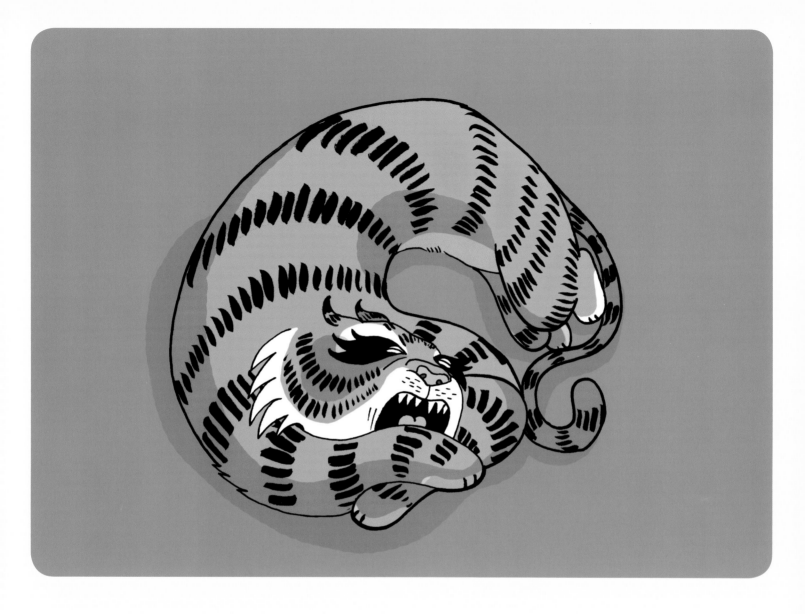

Tiger swaggered around Betty, mouth watering. "Stop the blah, blah, blah. I need a nap right now."

He was so tired from his journey, he started to snore almost immediately. When Betty saw that Tiger was asleep, she snuck out of the house.

When Tiger woke up, he was angry to find Betty gone. He yelled as he stamped down the road, "I'll be back. You better be here if you want to see your family again!"

Hiding in a big tree behind the house, Betty cried, "I must do something to save my family. But what can a little girl like me do?" A while later, she came up with a plan and decided to ask the people she trusted to help.

Running and running, with sweat on her face, she knocked on the door of Mr. Robinson, the town's tailor. She told him about Tiger.

Betty asked for a bag of needles to save her family. Mr. Robinson immediately gave her a bag of his biggest and sharpest needles.

Then Betty went to Mr. King, who kept many turtles as pets in his backyard. She told him about Tiger.

Betty asked for a hungry turtle to save her family.
Mr. King immediately gave her a huge hungry turtle.

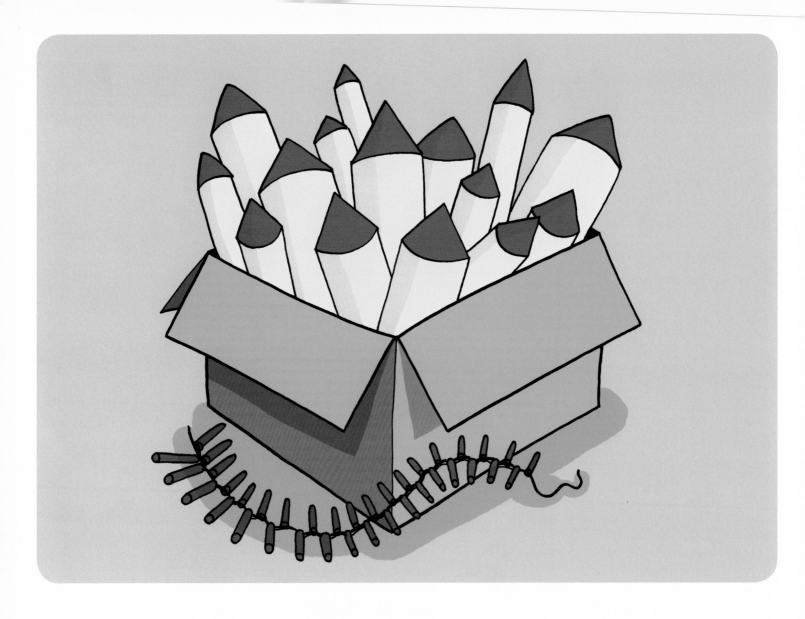

Finally, Betty knocked on the door of Mr. Sing, who sold fireworks for a living. She told him about Tiger.

Betty asked for some fireworks to save her family. Mr. Sing was hesitant at first. But after Betty explained how she was going to use them, he gave her a box of fireworks.

"Be careful anyway," he said, patting her head.

Betty dashed back home. She stuck the needles into the chair cushion. In the kitchen, she put the fireworks in the empty wood-burning stove.

Then she carefully placed the turtle inside the stove and removed all the light bulbs from the house. She smiled, feeling confident that she could defeat Tiger.

Soon after Betty hid herself in the tree, Tiger returned with Mommy and Penny. He tied them to the tree and then entered the house.

In the dark, Tiger sat down on the chair. Ouch!
He tried to turn on the light but nothing happened.
Letting out a squeal, he rushed into the kitchen to make a fire so
he could check on his behind.

When Tiger opened the stove door, the hungry turtle lumbered out and bit him. Ouch again!

After he finally lit the stove, the fireworks exploded and his tail caught fire.

"Roarrrrrrr!"

Tiger ran out of the house. The neighbors suddenly showed up to help. "Tiger! Tiger! Tail on fire!" they shouted as Tiger disappeared into the woods.

Everyone rejoiced. Mommy was so proud she cried tears of joy, and Penny wagged her tail and barked happily.

Betty giggled. "Who says I have to be big to be courageous?"

Lin was born in Hong Kong and now lives in New Jersey. A former banking professional, Lin has chosen to write children's book for the child she once was and still is at heart. Her diverse background gives her inspiration to focus on themes that open the hearts and minds of children from all cultures. Tiger! Tiger! Tail on Fire! is her third children's book.

Graphic Designer by day, illustrator by night, Ray credits many hot summers drawing caricatures at New Jersey theme parks for honing his illustration skills, which now have evolved into professional calling. He lives in Brooklyn, New York.